FAMILY PETS

OUR PET BIRD

by Michele Jakubowski
illustrated by Kev Payne

GRASSHOPPER

Tools for Parents & Teachers

Grasshopper Books enhance imagination and introduce the earliest readers to fiction with fun storylines and illustrations. The easy-to-read text supports early reading experiences with repetitive sentence patterns and sight words.

Before Reading

- Look at the cover illustration. What do readers see? What do they think the book will be about?
- Look at the picture glossary together. Sound out the words. Ask readers to identify the first letter of each vocabulary word.

Read the Book

- "Walk" through the book, reading to or along with the reader. Point to the illustrations as you read.

After Reading

- Review the picture glossary again. Ask readers to locate the words in the text.
- Ask the reader: If you had a pet bird, what would you teach it to say?

Grasshopper Books are published by Jump!
5357 Penn Avenue South
Minneapolis, MN 55419
www.jumplibrary.com

Library of Congress Cataloging-in-Publication Data

Names: Jakubowski, Michele, author.
Payne, Kev, 1978- illustrator.
Title: Our pet bird / by Michele Jakubowski;
illustrated by Kev Payne.
Description: Minneapolis, MN: Jump!, Inc., [2022]
Series: Family pets
Includes reading tips and supplementary back matter.
Audience: Ages 5-7.
Identifiers: LCCN 2020058526 (print)
LCCN 2020058527 (ebook)
ISBN 9781636901923 (hardcover)
ISBN 9781636901930 (paperback)
ISBN 9781636901947 (ebook)
Subjects: LCSH: Readers (Primary)
Parrots–Juvenile fiction.
Classification: LCC PE1119.2 .J35 2022 (print)
LCC PE1119.2 (ebook)
DDC 428.6/2–dc23
LC record available at https://lccn.loc.gov/2020058526
LC ebook record available at https://lccn.loc.gov/2020058527

Editor: Eliza Leahy
Direction and Layout: Anna Peterson
Illustrator: Kev Payne

Printed in the United States of America at
Corporate Graphics in North Mankato, Minnesota.

Table of Contents

Pete the Parakeet

"Hello!" says Pete the parakeet.

He can talk!

Pete rings a bell in his cage. He tweets. He lets us know he is awake.

“Can you say ‘Ben’?” I ask him. Ben is my name.

“Ben.” Grandma points at me.

“Ben,” Grandpa repeats. It helps Pete learn!

We clean Pete's cage
every morning.

Grandma fills his water.
Grandpa fills his food dish.

I give him a treat.
Bananas are
his favorite!

"Pretty bird!" I say.

Pete is happy.

He swings.
He looks
in his mirror.

"Pretty bird!"
he says.

We turn on music.
Pete tweets the tune.
He dances, too!

He flies around
the apartment.

At night, Pete sits on my shoulder. He listens while I read.

“The end,” I say. I close the book.

“The end, Ben!” says Pete.

Let's Review!

Some pet birds can learn to repeat words. Pete the parakeet learns some words. Which words did he say in the story?

A. Hello! **B.** Good night! **C.** Pretty bird! **D.** Treat, please!

Picture Glossary

apartment
A set of rooms to live in, usually rented and on one floor of a building.

favorite
The person or thing that you like more than all the others.

parakeet
A small parrot, often kept as a pet, with brightly colored feathers and a long, pointed tail.

tweets
Makes a short, high chirping sound.

Let's Review! Answer Key: **A.** Hello!, **C.** Pretty bird!